PANDORA

ARE YOU JUST A LITTLE BIT CURIOUS?

for Darcey

Shoo Rayner

Published by Shoo Rayner

www.shoorayner.com

ISBN 978-1-908944-405

Text and illustrations © Shoo Rayner 2018

The right of Shoo Rayner to be identified as the author and illustrator
of this work has been asserted by him in accordance with the
Copyright, Designs and Patents Act, 1988.

A CIP catalogue record for this book is available from the British Library.

With Thanks to my
cherished suppoters
on Kickstarter.com.

The Mirra Family
Angela Stanton
B P Moffit
Andreas Johansson
Diva Magpayo

Susanna Pitzer
Julian Assange
Chloé Mayol
Imke Spickenbom
Karen H Owens
Nancy Hemati
Thérèse Wijk

Maggie Hanshaw
Ceri Hunter
David Hanshaw
Mark & Allison Hodges
Carole Ann Howe
Pauline Reilly
James, Chloe, Jack, Lilly
Denis Sarrazin

Jeff Schinkel
Lisa Toole
Rose Tarrier
Ella Rayner
Greg Aldrich
Luke-Mark Williams
Elizabeth Jessica Anne Wood
Christopher, Jessica & Lucas Bardsley

Once upon a time, a long time ago, when everything was lovely and nothing bad had ever happened in the world, there was a very curious girl.

Her name was Pandora and she was curious about everything you can imagine.

She couldn't help herself.

That's just the way she was.

She was curious to know how lizards could walk on the ceiling.

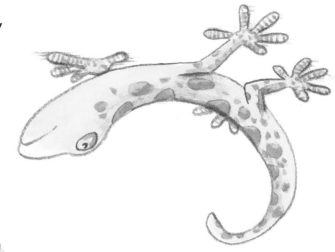

And why pomegranates had so many seeds.

And why the Sun didn't
burn holes in the sky.

And why the Moon chased
the stars all night.

Pandora was so curious that she mostly wanted to know about things that were absolutely none of her business.

More than anything else, she was curious about the room at the end of the long, dark corridor.

She had been told a **MILLION** times that she must never, ever go there, but she really was a very curious girl.

KEEP OUT!

So what do you think she did?

Of course! She did **EXACTLY** what she had been told she must **NEVER, EVER** do, even though she'd been told a **MILLION** times before.

She really was a very curious girl.

At midnight, when all the world was sleeping, Pandora took her lamp, with its flickety-flickering light, and she
SNICK,
SNACK,
SNUCK,
down
the stairs.

TIPPY,
TIPPY-TAP,
went her feet on
the floor, as she crept
down the long dark corridor.

Was she very naughty,
or was she just very curious?

The walls were painted with pictures of people.
Their eyes seemed to follow her,
WATCHING, WATCHING, WATCHING,
as she came to the end of the long, dark corridor.

THE LONG AND LONELY PITCH-DARK CORRIDOR,

where she stopped and reached out to open the door.

CLUNK! CLUNK! CLUNK!

Went the big, shiny handle.

SQUEAK! SQUEAK! sQUE-EE-EE-EE-EAK!

Went the hinges on the door.

BUMP!
BUMP!
BUMP!
Went Pandora's heart, as she silently tiptoed into the room.

It was cold in the room – FREEZING, FREEZING cold.
Pandora shivered and her breath made clouds.

She had been told a MILLION times before that she
must NEVER, EVER go there, but Pandora
really was a very, curious girl.

The room was almost empty.
A small wooden table stood on the plain, bare floor.
In the middle of the table sat a small wooden box.
A key lay by its side.

On the lid of the box were carved these words:

DO NOT
LOOK
INSIDE

Pandora couldn't help herself.
She really was a

VERY

curious
girl.

TICKETY! TICKETY! TICK!

Went the lizard on the ceiling.
It was the only sound in the quiet, quiet house.

SLIP! SLIP! SLIP!
Went the key into the lock

Do not look inside

CLICK! CLICK! CLICK!
The key turned so easily.

SLOWLY... SLOWLY... SLOWLY...

Pandora lifted up the lid of the box...

A cloud of horrid, nasty things flew from the box on rasping, buzzing wings.

Each little pest had a different name, like...

TROUBLE,

HUNGER,

FEAR,

AND SHAME.

They nipped and they bit and caught up in Pandora's hair.

Pandora ran like the wind.

The creatures followed in her wake, down the long, dark corridor and up, up, up the narrow, winding stairs.

In her room, they raced to the window, drawn by the darkness beyond, free at last to fill the world with all the bad and terrible things it had never known before.

Pandora dived beneath her bed-clothes, squeezed her eyes tight-shut, and scared herself to sleep!

The last of the creatures struggled to Pandora's room. It was different from all the others and went by the name of HOPE.

Drawing strength from the clear, bright light of the stars, it kissed and blessed the sleeping child, then it stretched its fluttering wings and went upon its way.

The very next day, a **MIRACLE** had happened!

Pandora was no longer quite so curious.
She stopped asking questions that did not concern her,
for she had learned an important lesson in life.

That it is almost always best
- if only you can remember -
to mind your own business,
and do as you are told!

Lightning Source UK Ltd.
Milton Keynes UK
UKHW052259230619

344891UK00001B/1/P

9 781908 944405